Logansport-Cass County Public Library

J 133.
Haunted places
Besel, Jennifer M., author.

HAUNTED PLACES

JEN BESEL

Black Rabbit Books

Bolt Jr. is published by Black Rabbit Books
P.O. Box 3263, Mankato, Minnesota, 56002.
www.blackrabbitbooks.com
Copyright © 2020 Black Rabbit Books

Grant Gould, designer; Omay Ayres, photo researcher

All rights reserved. No part of this book may be reproduced in any form without written permission from the publisher.

Names: Besel, Jennifer M., author.
Title: Haunted places / by Jen Besel.
Description: Mankato, MN : Black Rabbit Books, 2020. | Series: Bolt Jr. a little bit spooky | Includes bibliographical references and index.
Identifiers: LCCN 2019001000 (print) | LCCN 2019013547 (ebook) | ISBN 9781623101831 (ebook) | ISBN 9781623101770 (library binding) | ISBN 9781644661154 (paperback)
Subjects: LCSH: Haunted places—Juvenile literature. | Ghosts—Juvenile literature.
Classification: LCC BF1461 (ebook) | LCC BF1461 .B43 2020 (print) | DDC 133.1/2—dc23
LC record available at https://lccn.loc.gov/2019001000

Printed in the United States. 5/19

Image Credits
Alamy: Chris George Hughes, 12; Dale O'Dell, 16–17; destructoid.com: Chris Carter, 5; en.m.wikipedia.org: Alexander Gardiner/Christie's, 11 (Lincoln); Shutterstock: Aleksey Oleynikov, 20–21 (ghost); AlexLMX, 8–9 (camera); Alfredo Schaufelberger, 21 (inset); Anne Greenwood, 6–7; Baimieng, 10; breakermaximus, 8–9 (bkgd); Creaturart Images, 20–21 (cemetery); DreamLand Media, 18 (owl); Elena Schweitzer, 18 (house); Jannarong, 1; Joe Therasakdhi, 22–23; Late Night Rabbit, Cover; Mifid, 9 (motion detector); mipan, 9 (thermometer); Orhan Cam, 11 (White House); Razvan Ionut Dragomirescu, 4, 7 (inset); Suiraton, 13; szikszaizsu, 3, 14 (bkgd), 24; Valentyna7, 8 (recorder); Zacarias Pereira da Mata, 18 (ghost)

Contents

Chapter 1
Spooky Places 4

Chapter 2
Famous Spots 10

Chapter 3
Finding Answers 16

More Information 22

CHAPTER 1

Spooky Places

People walked through an old house. Suddenly, they heard **whispers**. They looked for who was speaking. But no one else was there. Was it a ghost?

whisper: words spoken very softly

5

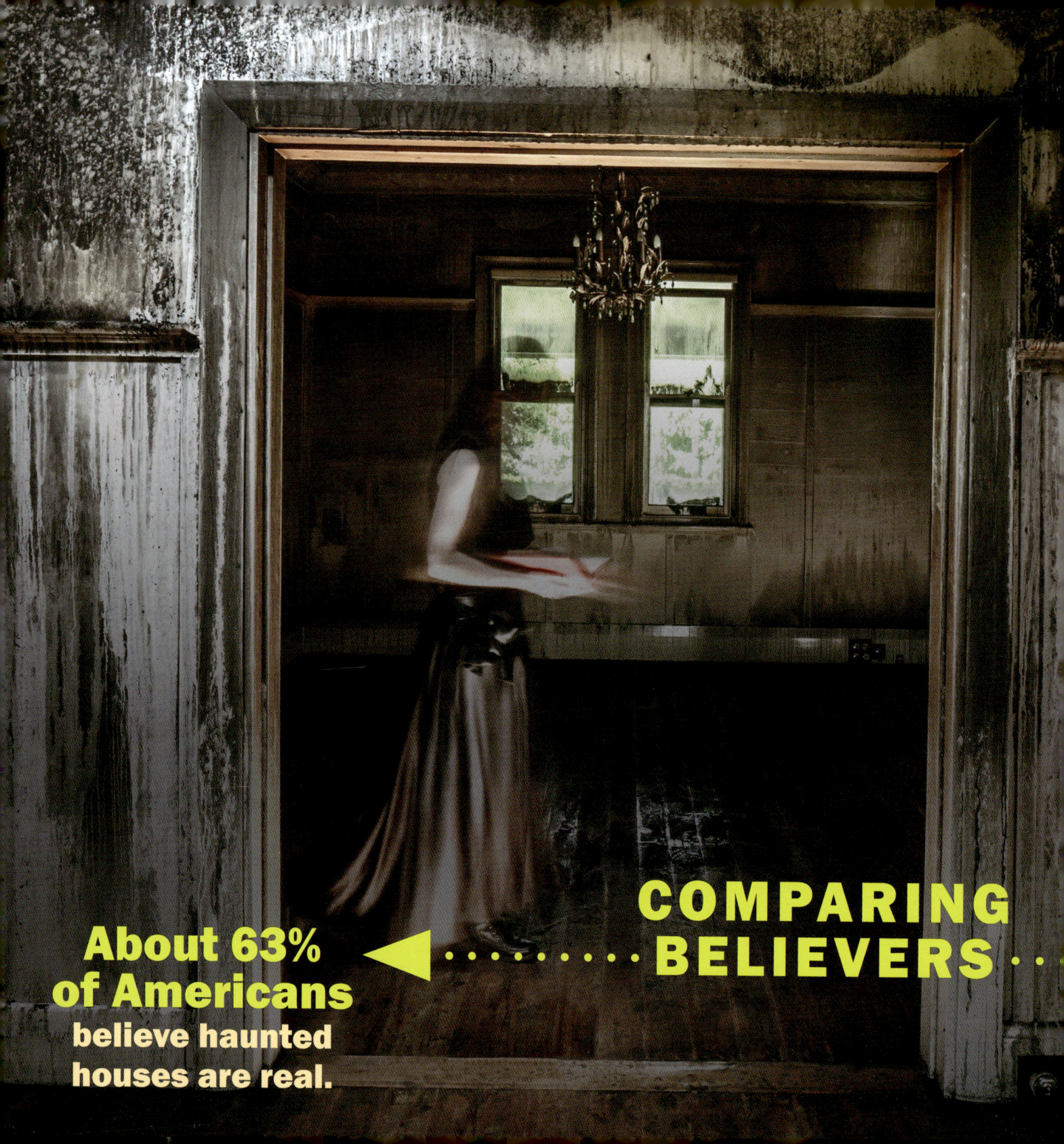

About 63% of Americans believe haunted houses are real.

COMPARING BELIEVERS

A Big Mystery

There are many stories about haunted places. Some people say they've seen ghosts. Others say they've heard spooky sounds. Ghost hunters look for answers. But no one knows if places are really haunted.

▶ **About 37% of Americans** don't believe in haunted houses.

TOOLS USED BY Ghost Hunters

recorder

video camera

thermometer

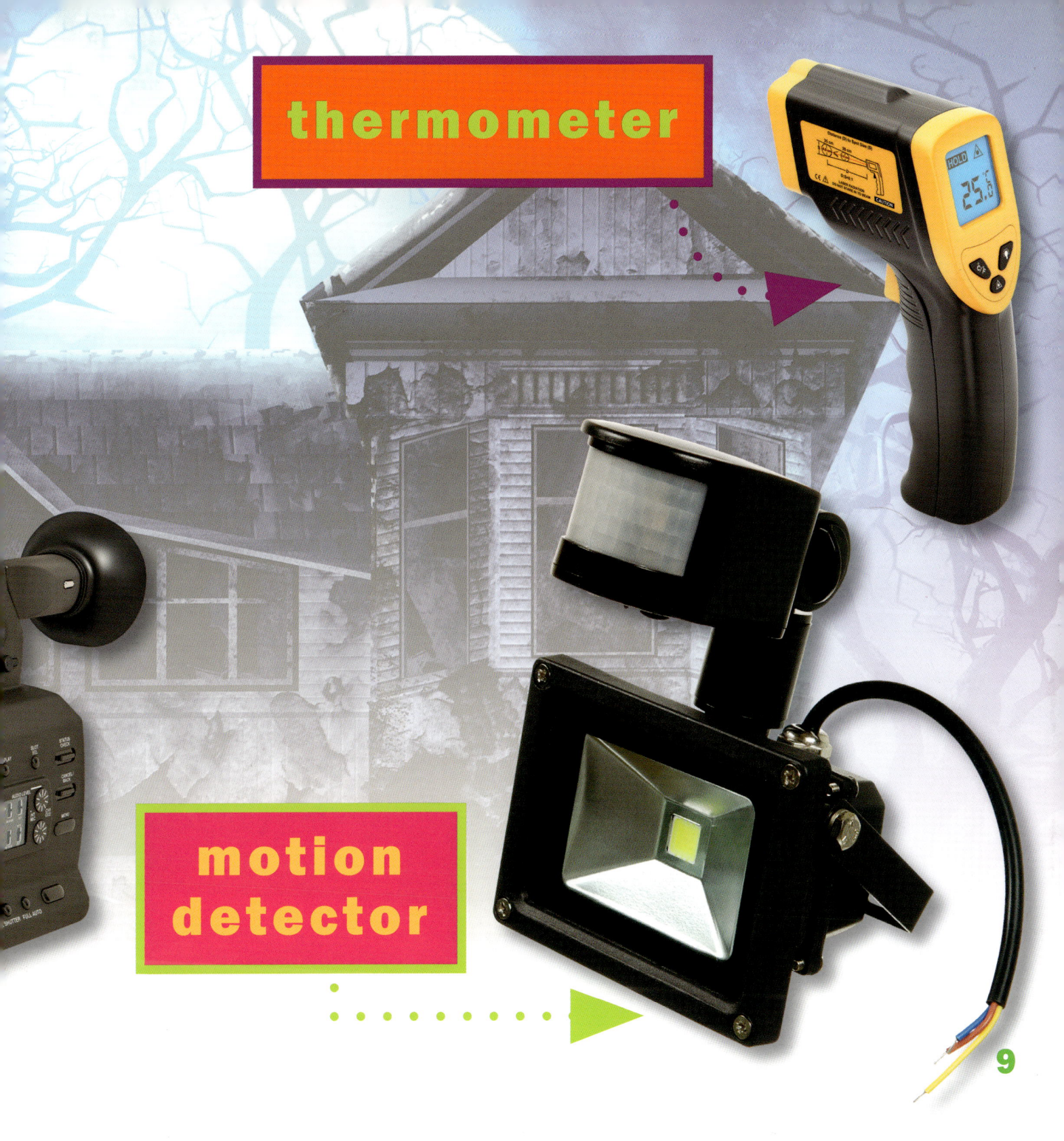

motion detector

9

CHAPTER 2

Famous Spots

Some places have many ghost stories. The **White House** is one of them. Many people say they saw **presidents'** ghosts there.

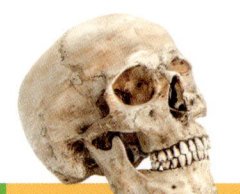

White House: where the U.S. president lives

president: a person who leads a government

FACT
One ghost might be Abraham Lincoln.

11

12

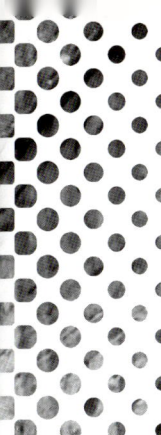

A Scary Prison

Alcatraz was a **prison**. Many men died there. Some think the men's ghosts are still there. People say they heard voices. Others saw ghosts.

prison: a place where criminals are held

Some Famous Haunted Places

Alcatraz in California

The White House in Washington, D.C.

Halifax Citadel in Nova Scotia

14

Tower of London in England

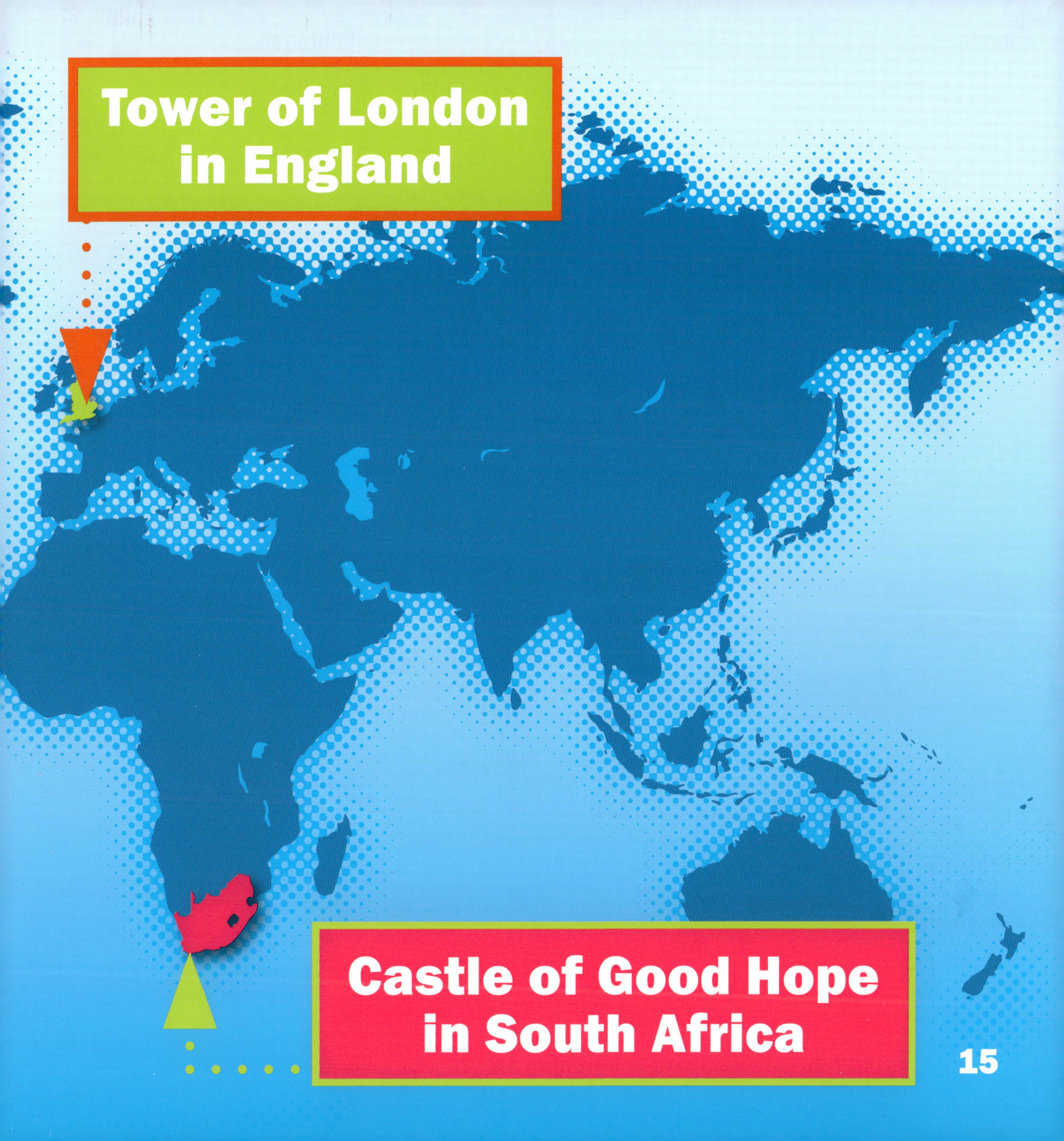

Castle of Good Hope in South Africa

15

CHAPTER 3

Finding Answers

Ghost hunters look for answers. They try to take pictures of ghosts. They also record sounds. Hunters say they've heard ghosts talk.

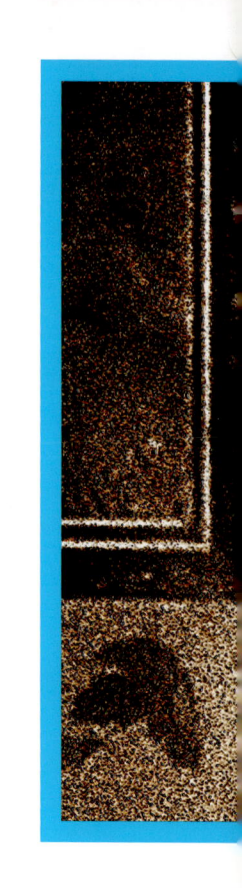

FACT Ghosts might cause cold spots.

Is that a face?

noises

white shapes

cold spots

Believe It or Not?

Many people think ghost stories are made-up. They think ghosts are shadows. The noises might be from wind. But others think something spooky is going on.

◀ • • • • • • • • • • • • • • **What Do You Think?**

Bonus Facts

People have told ghost stories for hundreds of years.

In pictures, **ghosts** might be circles of light.

Many movies are about haunted places.

Many ghost sightings are in cemeteries.

cemetery: a place where dead bodies are buried

READ MORE/WEBSITES

Bodden, Valerie. *Haunted Houses.* Creep Out. Mankato, MN: Creative Education, 2018.

Dolan, Elys. *The Mystery of the Haunted Farm.* Somerville, MA: Nosy Crow, an imprint of Candlewick Press, 2016.

Noll, Elizabeth. *Haunted Places.* Strange ... but True? Mankato, MN: Black Rabbit Books, 2017.

Ghosts
sd4kids.skepdic.com/ghosts

National Geographic Kids Weird But True Show - Haunted Houses!
soundcloud.com/siriusxmentertainment/national-geographic-kids-weird-but-true-show-haunted-houses

23

GLOSSARY

cemetery (SEM-uh-ter-ee)—a place where dead bodies are buried

president (PREZ-uh-dent)—a person who leads a government

prison (PRI-zuhn)—a place where criminals are held

whisper (WHIS-pur)—words spoken very softly

White House (WHITE HOWS)—where the U.S. president lives

INDEX

A
Alcatraz, 13, 14

G
ghost hunters, 7, 16

S
sounds, 4, 7, 13, 16

T
tools, 8–9

W
White House, 10, 14